D0574939

For Eleanor and George – *T.B.*
For Stephen, G, C, J and E – *S.G.*

Abridged by Rodney Kennard from *Old Peter's Russian Tales*, by Arthur Ransome (1916).

First published in Great Britain in 2005 by
Frances Lincoln Children's Books, 4 Torriano Mews,
Torriano Avenue, London NW5 2RZ
www.franceslincoln.com

Distributed in the USA by Publishers Group West

British Library Cataloguing in Publication Data
available on request

ISBN 1-84507-297-9

Set in Minion

Printed in China
1 3 5 7 9 8 6 4 2

Little Daughter of the Snow

Arthur Ransome

Edited by Shena Guild
Illustrated by Tom Bower

FRANCES LINCOLN CHILDREN'S BOOKS

There was once an old man and an old woman, his wife. They lived in a village on the edge of the forest. They had dogs and a cat and roosters and hens, but they had no children – and this made them very sad.

The old people would stand for hours, peeping through the window to watch other people's children playing outside. In winter, the children played in the crisp snow, pelting each other with snowballs or rolling snow together to make a Baba Yaga – a snow witch.

One day, the old man said, "Wife, let us go into the yard and make a little snow girl. Perhaps she will come alive and be a little daughter to us."

The two old people put on their big fur coats and went out into the yard. Tenderly they rolled up the snow and began to make a little snow girl.

Towards evening, when they finished, she was more beautiful than you could ever imagine – a little girl, all snow, with sparkling white eyes, and a little mouth, with snow lips tightly closed.

"Oh, speak to us," begged the old man.

"Won't you run about like the others, little white pigeon?" cried the old woman.

Suddenly, in the twilight, her eyes shone blue like the sky on a clear day. Her lips opened and she smiled. Her hair was black and stirred in the wind.

The little girl began dancing in the snow like a little white spirit, tossing her long hair and laughing. Her eyes shone, and while the old people watched her and wondered and thanked God, she sang:

"No warm blood in me doth glow,
Water in my veins doth flow;
Yet I'll laugh and sing and play
By frosty night and frosty day –
Little Daughter of the Snow.

But whenever I do know
That you love me little, then
I shall melt away again.
Back into the sky I'll go –
Little Daughter of the Snow."

"Isn't she beautiful!" said the old man. He picked up the snow girl, and she put her little cold arms around his neck.

"You must not keep me too warm," she said.

The old woman made her a little coat, and the old man bought her a little fur hat, and red boots. Then they dressed the little snow girl.

"Too hot, too hot!" she said. "I must go out into the cool night."

"But you must go to sleep now," said the old woman.

"By frosty night and frosty day," sang the little girl, "I am the Little Daughter of the Snow. I will play by myself in the yard all night, and in the morning I will play with the other children."

All night she danced in the moonlight, chasing her shadow and throwing snowballs at the stars. In the morning she came in, laughing, to have breakfast with the old people. She showed them how to make porridge for her. All they needed was a piece of ice crushed in a wooden bowl.

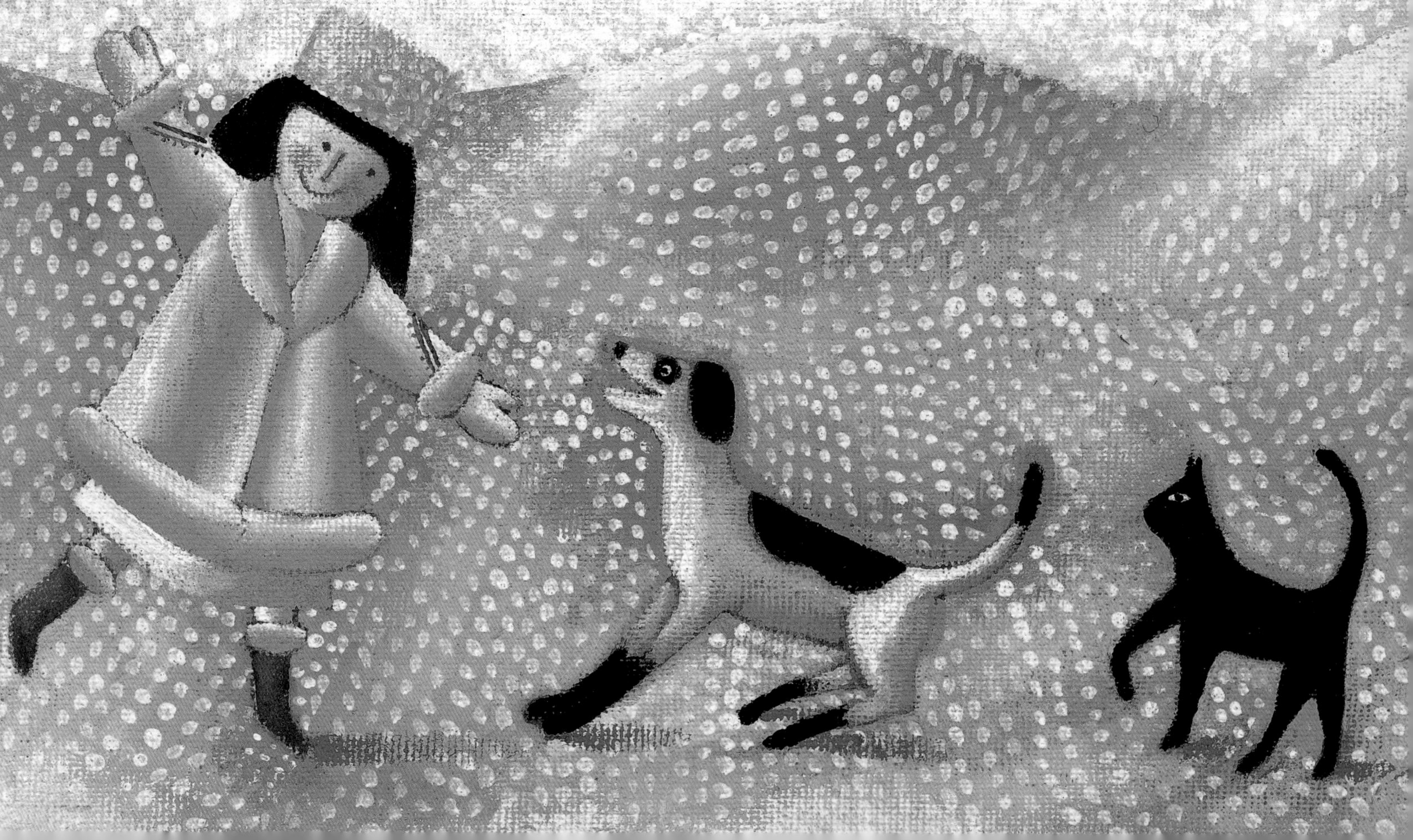

After breakfast the snow girl ran out to play with the other children. She could run faster than any of them. Her little red boots flashed as she ran about. The old people watched her proudly.

"She is all our own," said the old woman.

"Our little white pigeon," said the old man.

In the evening she had another bowl of ice-porridge, and went off to play by herself in the snow again.

And so it went on all through the winter, the little snow girl singing and laughing and dancing. She would do everything the old people told her, except sleep indoors.

All the children in the village loved her.

And so came the end of winter. The snow melted, and people could go out on the paths once more. Often the children would go a little way into the forest. The little snow girl always went with them – it would have been no fun without her.

One day, they went too far into the wood.

But when the children said they were going to turn back, the little snow girl tossed her head and ran on, laughing. The others were afraid to follow her. It was getting dark. They waited for her as long as they dared, and then they ran home.

The little snow girl was lost in the forest, all alone.

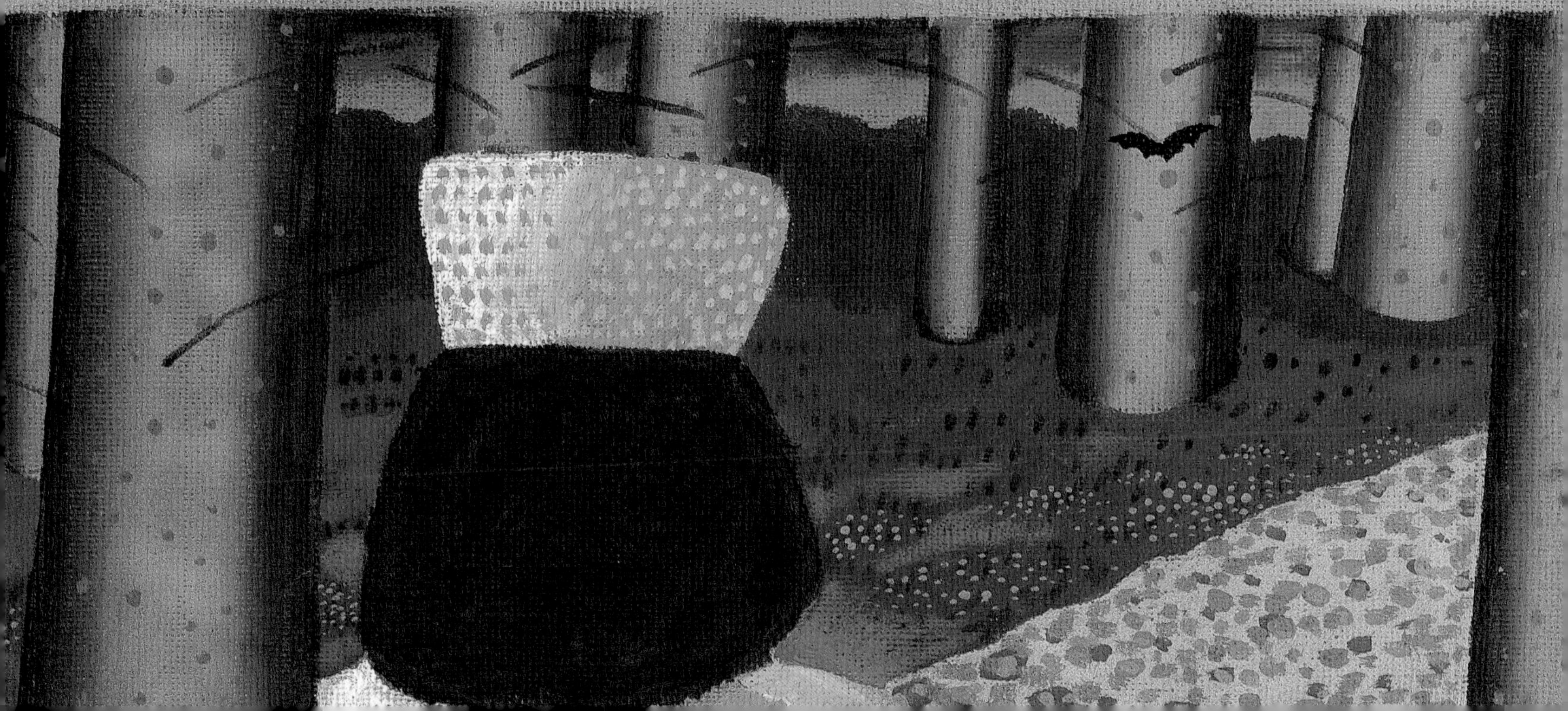

She climbed up into a tree, but could see no further than when she was on the ground.

"Little friends, little friends, where are you?" she called out from the tree.

A big brown bear heard her, and came shambling up on his heavy paws.

"What are you crying about, Little Daughter of the Snow?"

"Brown bear," she said, "I have lost my way, and dusk is falling, and all my little friends are gone."

"I will take you home," said the bear.

"Brown bear, I am afraid of you. I think you would eat me. I would rather go home with someone else."

So the bear shambled away.

An old grey wolf heard her, and came running up on swift feet.

"Why are you crying, Little Daughter of the Snow?"

"Grey wolf," said the little girl, "I have lost my way, and it is getting dark, and all my little friends have gone."

"I will take you home," said the wolf.

"Grey wolf, I am afraid of you. I think you would eat me. I would rather go home with someone else."

So the wolf ran away.

An old red fox heard her, and came up to the tree.

"Why are you crying, Little Daughter of the Snow?"

"Red fox," said the little girl, "I have lost my way, and it is dark, and all my little friends have gone."

"I will take you home," said the fox.

"Red fox, I am not afraid of you. I will go home with you."

The little snow girl scrambled down the tree. She held the fox by the hair of his back as he ran through the dark forest. Soon they saw lights, and in a few minutes they were at the door of the old man and the old woman.

There were the old people, crying,
“Oh, what has become of our little snow girl?”
“Oh, where is our little white pigeon?”

“Here I am!” called the little snow girl. “The kind red fox has brought me home.”

“We are very grateful to you,” the old man said to the fox.

“Are you really?” said the red fox, “for I am very hungry.”

“Here is a nice crust for you,” said the old woman.

“What I would like,” said the fox, “is a nice plump hen. Your little snow girl is worth a nice plump hen.”

The old woman agreed. But she grumbled to her husband, “It seems a waste to give away a good plump hen.”

“It does,” he said, and then the old woman told him what she meant to do.

Into one sack they put a fine plump hen, and into another, they put the fiercest of their dogs. They took the two bags outside and called to the fox.

The old red fox came up, licking his lips. They opened one sack, and out fluttered the hen. Then, just as the fox was about to seize her, they opened the other sack, and out jumped the fierce dog, eyes flashing. The poor fox was so frightened that he ran back into the forest.

"Now we have our little snow girl," said the old man and the old woman, "and we have not had to give away our nice plump hen."

Then they heard the little snow girl, singing:

"Old ones, old ones, now I know
Less you love me than a hen,
I shall go away again.
Good-bye, ancient ones, good-bye,
Back I go across the sky;
To my motherkin I go –
Little Daughter of the Snow."

They ran into the hut. There, in front of the stove, was a pool of water, a fur hat, a little coat and little red boots. Yet it seemed that they saw the little snow girl, with her bright eyes and long hair, dancing in the room.

"Don't go! Don't go!" they begged. Already they could hardly see her. But they heard her laughing and her song:

"...to my motherkin I go –
Little Daughter of the Snow."

Just then, the door blew open. A cold wind filled the room, and the Little Daughter of the Snow was gone.

She leapt into the arms of Frost, her father, and Snow, her mother, and they carried her high up over the stars to the far north. There she plays all through the year on the frozen seas, the Little Daughter of the Snow.